# The Waiting List

## AN IRAQI WOMAN'S TALES OF ALIENATION

Modern Middle East
Literatures in Translation
Series

# The Waiting List

AN IRAQI WOMAN'S TALES OF ALIENATION

## Daisy Al-Amir

Translated from Arabic by Barbara Parmenter

Introduction by Mona Mikhail

Center for Middle Eastern Studies
The University of Texas at Austin

Library of Congress Catalogue Card Number: 94-72717

ISBN 0-292-79067-8

Printed in the United States of America

**Cover photograph**: Caroline Williams

**Drawings**: Douglas Rugh

**Cover design**: Diane Watts

**Formatting**: Virginia Howell

**Editor and book designer**: Annes McCann-Baker

Distributed by arrangement with University of Texas Press/Box 7819
Austin, Texas 78713

# Table of Contents

# Acknowledgments

Members of the Center were fortunate to meet distinguished Iraqi author Daisy Al-Amir when she was in the States in 1989. At that time, Elizabeth Fernea introduced us to her and to her many collections of short stories. *Ala La'hat al Intizar* was her latest Arabic publication at that time, and we agreed to have Arabic translation expert Barbara Parmenter translate the stories into English for publication in the Modern Middle East Literatures in Translation Series as soon as possible.

Daisy returned to Lebanon, but continued to help us with the translation and the choice of illustrations. We were fortunate to be able to hire Doug Rugh, a graduate of the Rhode Island School of Design, to draw our illustrations of the stories, and Middle Eastern architectural scholar Caroline Williams agreed to let us use her photograph of the Beirut coastline as a cover illustration. Mona Mikhail, author and scholar of Arabic literature, has written our fine Introduction. Thus, through another international collaboration of effort was the Center able to bring *The Waiting List*, number 16 in the Series, to the attention of the English-speaking public.

Annes McCann-Baker
Editor
Center for Middle Eastern Studies
The University of Texas at Austin

# Author's Preface

In the experience of any artist, there is stage prior to the beginning of production, and then the first stage of the productive period. Periods of ebb and flow follow next, surging or retreating in response to experiences, during which the creative urge might dwindle to a virtual halt or continue to rise.

I wrote my first story in Lebanon in 1962, and published it in the Lebanese magazine *al-Adab*. Before this story, I had never before attempted to write, never torn up rough drafts nor even given a thought to writing.

In each issue, *al-Adab* ran a column critiquing stories published in the previous issue. In the issue following the appearance of my story, there was a favorable review, and then came a succession of articles inquiring about my background and if I had previously published stories. It may appear from this that success in writing was easy, but, to take a step backwards, I must say that this success did not come out of a vacuum. Before I wrote, published, succeeded, and became a known writer, I had passed through many experiences which deeply affected my life and through which I lived by give and take.

As a young person I read every book that fell into my hands, and yet reading did not inspire me to write. My days as a student were richly productive, especially at the university. Then came a successful teaching career, which enabled me to take many trips during the school holidays. As a tourist I never stayed long in the countries I observed.

Before these clearly classifiable periods, I used to move with my family between Iraqi provinces in accordance with my father's work as a doctor. This mobility forced me into a period of psychological weaning, more difficult than my young age could endure. The loss of familiarity with places, friends, and schools was more than my psyche could accept.

The hardest stage of this weaning came the day I left Baghdad to live in Basra. Later I left Basra for an uncertain future. There was a period of study in Britain that lasted more than a year, during which I came to understand the feeling of alienation one experiences in foreign lands and what it means to depend on myself alone, to long for home, and to be exposed to new and unfamiliar social concepts and conventions. In 1960 I arrived in Lebanon and it was decided for me that I should stay there. I felt that my psyche had been deluged, that I knew the facts of life, and that I had discovered by myself through varying experiences of fear, joy, curiosity, alienation, contentment, anger, and anxiety, truths to which I had never been introduced in all my reading and studies and professional activities as a teacher.

In fact these truths became the deep-rooted foundation onto which settled new experiences and the discoveries I would make from them.

All this interplay between events of the distant past and the new present, mingling and fragmenting, emerged in that first short story which marked a new stage in my life. I had become a writer.

I wrote other stories, and in 1964 I was able to publish my first collection entitled *The Distant Land You Love* (three printings). The title carried the meaning of all the memories and longings, scattered here and there among the places I knew inside and outside of Iraq. Although I treasured these memories, I also felt them as an unwanted burden bearing down on me.

At that time I was past my youth and at a mature age, able to balance between mind and emotions. This balance applied to all the heroines of my stories. Personal affairs no longer took first place in my concerns. I rejoiced or grieved for both specific and general reasons, but the specific always sparked my interest in the general.

My stay in Lebanon lasted more than a quarter of a century, but most of the time I was on Iraqi territory, working in our embassy. I was not an émigré, nor an exile, and never far from this piece of my homeland inside Lebanon.

This merging of Iraq and Lebanon, with all its memories coming to and from the self, gave me a huge store of ideas, meanings, and concepts which increased every day through new excursions, discoveries, friendships, and extensive conversations with artists, philosophers, writers, and politicians.

In this rich and giving atmosphere, there was in my soul an apprehension about not having a stable home. One day, I knew, my diplomatic posting would have to come to an end, and the Iraqi government would order me home. Yet, this lack of stability provided me with heightened experiences because I was always in a state of nervous readiness to return. I came to feel that every day was a new experience.

During this period I published a collection of stories entitled *And Then the Wave Returned* (1969, three printings). An Arab critic commented about my work, "This author has no house. Her main character is the car or the street." In 1975, I published the collection *The Happy Arab House* (five printings).

The Arab critic was correct. I had been living with my father's wife, but when my father died I decided to live by myself. My private wars ended, but the Lebanese war began. I published a collection of stories entitled, *In the Vortex of Love and Hate* (two printings) about the Lebanese war. Economic and emotional independence gave me the strength which enabled me to face all manner of difficulties. I had become master of my self, making my own decisions in my personal affairs. I live alone with no guardian over me, and I ask no favors from anyone. Yet if a woman lives alone she must sometimes ask for help in the course of her daily activities, and this help may expose her to gossip and rumors, and may shake her self-confidence. Here I go back to what I said before about how necessary it is to balance between the mind and emotions in order to continue living by give and take. By take, I mean winning the respect and concern of others, for other people, whether we like it or not, are the driving force in the tumultuous din of life's confusing labyrinth.

The experiences through which I passed were stored inside my soul. My memories are a storehouse of the past for which no key is needed—it opens automatically whenever I begin to write. The present ignites the need to write, while the future offers a goal.

Personal struggle and victory, and our efforts to preserve these, impel and prepare us to write. The life path an artist lives, no matter how exhausting, is the unceasing experience not only of one's own affairs but of others.

In 1971, I published a collection entitled, *Promises for Sale* (two printings). The heroine in this collection is a strong and resolute woman who determines her own fate without fear, confident in the correctness of her choices.

My stories have been met with interest since I started publishing, and even before my first collection appeared. They have been translated into a number of languages, and are studied at universities by specialists in Arabic, and in translation as a part of modern world literature.

This is a rosy picture of my career, but its other face involved loss, fear, confusion, and dashed hopes. I was successful by my own efforts outside the house, yet, inside, I never felt at home. I lost all sense of peace when my mother died while I was still in school. My family was small and we had to split up after my mother's passing. Although I lived with my siblings, I felt no buttress protecting me against life's surprises.

Solitude became my companion, but I tried consciously to distance myself from alienation. A mood of sadness permeated everything I wrote, not out of pessimism, but because my inner radar invariably honed in on sorrow. It picked up simple, insignificant incidents which in turn became the events around which my stories revolved. The main character was always a woman because I understand women more then men, although they certainly both play their roles to perfection on life's stage—men with false bravado and women with chronic fear.

When I returned to Iraq in 1985, the war with Iran was still going on, and our victories continued. Except for two stories, I was unable to involve myself with the war enough to write fiction about it. I did write dozens of fragments of literary prose, but fiction requires that events be stored, aged, and experienced over a long time, to be explored and revealed in a personal way. If I had been a poet, my prose fragments might have been expressed in verse.

The greatest emotional weaning I attempted was to forget Lebanon. I don't believe in allegiance to a country other than one's native land, and yet I was unable and unwilling to cancel with a stroke of the pen a quarter of a century of experience, the most beautiful period of my life. Lebanon taught me so much—it gave and I took, though I could offer only affection and devotion in return.

This struggle between trying to forget and trying to reacclimate to my homeland was the subject explored by events in my sixth collection of stories, *On the Waiting List*, published in 1988 (two printings). Both Lebanon and Iraq played major parts in this collection, which opened a vast storehouse of the past, the contents of which had long been out of sight, yet had not faded.

Now I have come to see reading as an escape from memories which are useless to recall. I find in reading novels and stories prefabricated revelations uncovered by their authors. I've reached a level where I understand life through my own experience, and that is what I write about rather than the experiences of others in their particular situations, places or perspectives.

After *On the Waiting List*, I wrote other stories which dealt with my personal fears. Solitude was no longer a companion—it now filled me with a frightening, repulsive sense of alienation.

These days, however, I no longer want to write about my personal anxieties, which I didn't write about when I first started. It seems I'm in a shell now and I must leap out.

I fear silence lest it persist and I find myself unable to speak at all. The store house of the past is nearly depleted, and, as for the present, I can't buy experiences to fill it nor force them to come to me. As for forcing myself to write, it is of no use because the creative act springs from a place we don't understand, and with a strength we can't resist, in images and details we thought we had long ago forgotten. Forcing the pen to write is failure, and I don't wish to surrender to failure. My love of life, my strength in bearing its difficulties, my personal independence, my discoveries of life's secrets—these were my capital. What is left to me from these funds by which I knew myself and by which others knew me? I am searching for a spring to fill my flask of experience. But how can I find a spring like this, which is the exact opposite of the routine I now live?

I want the spring to be as near and deep as the other springs that have given me sustenance and made me a serene artist true to herself and to others. I wish to hurry my arrival lest my thoughts dry up and my prayers for their return remain unheard. How can I reconcile that past sense of self with the present self who feels lost and abandoned? Who will keep that sense of loss at bay?

This is the struggle—I don't know what is emotionally true and what is intellectually true. I have lost my way in the labyrinths of emotion and intellect, and I beg to find the balance I once boasted about and which saved me from ruin and alienation. I am a person and an instrument at the same time, so how do I stand between these two aspects of myself? Where am I now in relation to all I know and all I have discovered? What use is swimming in the sea without a dream of seeing the horizon!

Baghdad
Autumn, 1989

## Author's Update

Back in Iraq, I felt as if I were living under a blockade because travel was forbidden for Iraqis. For five years I was trapped in these circumstances, and this siege mentality became the subject of my writing. Then suddenly the government exempted me from the travel ban, and I was able to accept an invitation to visit the United States from Dr. Miriam Cooke, chair of the Arabic Department at Duke University in North Carolina. This invitation delivered me from my severe emotional crisis. After visiting Duke, I traveled to several other universities where I found that I was already well-known in academic circles.

The Gulf War broke out during my visit, making it impossible to return to Iraq, and for a year and a half I stayed in America. There, I experienced things I had never known before. I once again lived with family, in this case my sister's grown children in Houston, who showered me with the utmost kindness, love and generosity. And yet I felt ill at ease, as I was accustomed to living on my own as an emotionally and financially independent woman. Houston was new and foreign to me, and I was tired of hearing news about the war.

Finally, in August, 1991, I returned to Beirut. I had left my house there in the care of friends. The civil war had left it in ruins, its furnishings broken and useless. With great pain, I accomplished the daunting task of helping my friends to move out. Then, with the help of my sister's children once again, I repaired the structure and brought in enough new furniture to make it fit for daily living. This entire experience, however, profoundly changed my feelings towards Lebanon—it was no longer the place I had once loved so much. It also transformed my emotional state. Whereas in America I had written about alienation and exile, in Lebanon I began to write stories filled with the taste of death. I am preparing these new stories for publication as a collection entitled *Plastic Surgery for Time*. In this way I have once again begun to write, tapping on new experiences now filling in my life's storehouse of memories.

For the time being, I am living in Lebanon, but planning to return to Iraq at some point. As usual, I cannot tell what the future will bring. For me that is the eternal question, always pressing on my mind, exhausting my emotions, terrifying my soul.

Beirut
March, 1994

# Introduction

It is a relatively recent phenomenon that English translations of writings by Arab women are being published in the West, so this collection is certainly a welcome addition to this growing library. Aside from the well known Iraqi woman poet Nazik al-Malaika, credited for playing a leading role in the free-verse movement along with her countryman the famous Badr Shakir al-Sayyab, little has been published in English about Iraqi contributions to contemporary Arabic literature. With this selection of stories, Daisy al-Amir receives a long overdue recognition of her talent and creativity.

"Woman must write herself...Woman must put herself into the text as into the world and into history by her movement," wrote Helene Cixous in her manifesto on *ecriture feminine*, *The Laugh of the Medusa*. Daisy al-Amir, a distinguished Iraqi woman writer, is doing precisely this, "putting herself into her texts." With this highly individualistic yet universal view point, she shapes for herself a lasting place among the growing crop of writers, poets and novelists of her country, and within the select group of Arab women writers at large.

As part of an elite educated group, al-Amir, along with several Iraqi writers, investigates in her stories the pressures of Iraqi ideology among other topics. For, these writers see their commitment both as a challenge to history and a solemn duty necessary in times of social crises.

Daisy al-Amir, along with other leading Iraqi authors, sees herself engaged in the struggles she portrays. In many ways these writers are the true heroes and heroines of their novels.

To better understand the cultural and socio-political background against which the writings of authors like Daisy al-Amir can be rightly assessed, we may look at some historical facts surrounding the emergence of contemporary Iraqi fiction.

Very often, the fall of the monarchy, and the dismantling of the feudal system and the rise of the 1958 revolution are quoted as the pivotal events that have helped shape Iraq's destiny in the last four decades or so.

Prior to the recent Gulf War, Iraq was also positioning itself as one of the leading patrons of the arts within the Arab world. For instance, the Iraqi government had earmarked large funds from its oil revenues to support and sponsor symposia, conferences, art exhibits and festivals both inside and outside of its country. There was a time when Iraq was also sponsoring the publication of a large and varied number of literary and artistic magazines, which attracted the contribution of some of the best Arab authors, critics and journalists, and in some cases leading foreign contributors as well.

The Babylon Art Festival and the Marbid Literary Festival for instance were but two of the well established artistic events that yearly drew hundreds of participants to this Arab capital which was lavishly trying to recreate its past glories. It had also established the highly coveted Saddam Hussein Literary Prize.

Poetry has traditionally been the dominating literary genre in Iraq. In the early twentieth century, Iraq had produced such towering figures as al-Rusafi, and al-Zahawi, to be followed by such influential poets as Nazik al-Malai'ka, Badr Shakir al-Sayyab, Buland al-Haydari, and Abdel Wahhab al-Bayati, who have revolutionized Arabic poetry and still continue to exert their influence on the younger generation of poets.

When we turn to fiction, we note that the novel and short story, as new genres have only begun to take their legitimate place on the Arab literary scene in the last twenty years or so.

Most critics agree that up to the Revolution of 1958, Iraqi prose writers were producing literature of uneven quality. The noted Iraqi critic Muhsin al-Mussawi commented that with the fall of the monarchy, the dismantling of the feudal system, and the rise of the Baath Party, new parameters for Iraqi fiction began to emerge. Early experimentations in novel writing were constrained by the notion of depicting the trials and tribulations of individual protagonists. Then the writers gradually and successfully ventured into creating larger numbers of characters, all the while maintaining their individualities. The multiple protagonists began to forcefully voice their views on politics, love and sex. That was a radical move from the traditional early novels and short stories which had uniformally used the undifferentiated voice of the author. Iraqi fiction comes into its own by creating a multiplicity of voices, well orchestrated as we note in the works of the writers of the seventies and eighties.

Emerging from a feudal society and getting their first exposures to the West, young Iraqi writers would often embark on writing careers upon their return to their native Iraq. These early attempts often took the form of didactic tracts, calling for reforms and challenging traditional structures, and were clearly influenced by some of the other Arab writers such as Abbas Mahmoud al-Aqqad, Ibrahim al-Mazini, Salama Musa, Taha Husayn and, more recently, Naguib Mahfouz and Yusuf Idris.

Their writings were also reflective of British, French and Russian influences. There were also some attempts at reviving and drawing upon the Arab literary heritage, by incorporating narrative forms drawn from folk epics such as *Gilgamesh, Siras,* or the *Alf Layla wa Layla* (The Thousand and One Nights).

Similar to the course of development in other Arab countries, the early experimentation at prose fiction writing took the form of serialized installments of *roman feuillton* type of dramatic literature. These were typically highly melodramatic, romantic and often unrealistic stories.

It is only in the early forties that we begin to read writers who handle reality and fiction in more meaningful ways.

Dhu al-Nun Ayub, born in 1908, is one of the early pioneers of Iraqi fiction. His celebrated novel *Al-Duktur Ibrahim* is an Iraqi classic. It is the saga of one of those "hollow intellectuals," who upon returning from his academic sojourns in England, like so many Iraqis and Arabs do, becomes an exploitative and somewhat tyrannical intellectual in power. Disillusioned and embittered, he prefers to return to the West rather than struggle to bring about the dreamed-of changes.

Dhu al Nun Ayub wrote this novel in 1939, and proceeded to write more works that dealt with similar bourgeois intellectuals who flirt with revolutionary ideas but turn into parasites and tyrants. Alienation and disillusionment became the trademark of most of these heroes.

These works thus addressed with great courage endemic questions that beleaguered Arab societies. Ayub has often been dubbed as the pioneer of social realism in the novel in Iraq. His collection, *The Toilers,* was dedicated to the masses of peasants and workers. Another memorable collection, *The Tower of Babel,* harps on the endemic corruption among the Iraqi middle class and resonates with irony.

Another Iraqi writer who made a name for himself and who is of similar background is Abdel Malik Nouri, born in 1921. He and Fouad al Tekirli studied and practiced law. Nouri went on to become a judge and resorted to the use of symbolism and allegory in attempts at evading the scrutiny of censorship.

The decades of the fifties and sixties reflect more poignantly the polemics and controversies that have dominated the Arab world. A salient theme in recent Iraqi writings is the aftermath of the 1967 setback, forcefully expressing disenchantment with ruling regimes and the endemic lack of freedom in societies. Intellectuals, as portrayed for instance in Abd al-Rahman al-Rubayi's novel *Al-Washm* (The Tattoo), are totally disillusioned and alienated from their society and are left aimless at the end of the novel.

Iraq has also adopted some other Arab writers such as the Palestinian Jabra Ibrahim Jabra and the Saudi Abd Al-Rahman Munif, who have gained fame and recognition both in the Arab world and in the West.

*Ala La'hat al Intizar* (On the Waiting List) is in some ways a refreshing departure from these themes. Here we are introduced into the highly private lives of heroines and heroes and invited to scrutinize their innermost feelings about simple incidents that take on highly charged meanings. Al-Amir partakes of all that her compatriots experience, of loss and alienation but gives an added personal dimension that is uniquely discernible as her voice. Ghada al-Samaan the well known Syrian novelist, put it succinctly when she stated:

> As an Arab citizen, a woman suffers from all the constraints imposed on any of her compatriots...in addition the attempt by women to restore their rights is part of the attempt by Arab individuals to restore their very humanity. (*al-Qabila tastajwib al-Qatila*, Ghada Samaan, 1981.)

Poignant questions besiege al-Amir's characters and pose a very intimate look at the inner workings of Arab individuals, mainly women, operating in an urban environment. It is the city and very often a foreign locale that operates as the backdrop for most of her stories and seems to mold the reactions of its protagonists. *On the Waiting List* has several of the stories taking place specifically in and around airports. Her protagonists seem to be constantly on the move, be it loitering in airports of moving from one location to another, always being threatened by losing touch with their roots. There is a lingering nostalgia for the past, as poignantly portrayed in the story "Thaman Bakhis" (For a Pittance). This story in many ways encapsulates the salient theme within this short collection. "In my travels I came to an unfamiliar city." Once in the faceless and nameless city, she searches for connections and in this case finds them in the unwanted memorabilia of a "weighty past" enfolded in a discarded picture album that no one seemed to want. She salvages the memories of those unknown individuals by buying that collection and tries to reconstruct the past of these relationships of seemingly "three generations" that made up the family that had sold "its past."

Michelle Murray, poet and novelist, in her introduction to the edited collection of essays *A House of Good Proportion*, points out that "Woman begins to be problematical to herself and others when her consciousness develops to a point where she sees herself as entitled to an individual life rather than to an impersonal predestination" (page 20). It seems that this is precisely what Daisy al-Amir is accomplishing in her stories.

Whether she uses the narrative "I" or the conventional third person, al-Amir is transparently narrating her present itinerant reality. She seems to be constantly roaming the globe, on a "waiting list" or pondering on papers from "ancient archives." Visiting and revisiting is also a dominant movement in these stories. Be it a "small notebook with yellowed papers" or "masses of letters," she is immersed in a past but also summoned to a poignant present which is forever changing. In "Fires of the Past" she puts it succinctly: "Yet she had never stayed in one house, and settling had not been part of her life."

"Doctor's Prescription" is another story which is telegraphically delivered with great economy. It is representative of Daisy al-Amir's economical style. There is virtually no redundancy in her narration, no repetitiveness but rather stark, denuded prose which hits its mark forcefully.

In what one may describe as vignettes, or impersonal dialogues, she investigates other narrative possibilities for transmitting her message. In a running repartee, which is faceless and nameless (a devise now widely used by several Arab women writers and journalists particularly in women's magazines), Al-Amir probes into the intricacies of human relations between husband and wife. At times these vignettes resonate with lyrical tones. A certain minimalism and terseness in her style speaks directly and convincingly to a hurried and on-the-go urbanized reader, who is probably also on a "waiting list" at a Waq Waq airport.

Mona Mikhail
New York University
1994

*Autumn's Umbrella*

# Autumn's Umbrella

Although the clouds were not thick they lay low, nearly touching the roofs. Yet the morning was not cold. It was autumn, deep and ambiguous, and its bittersweet sadness pierced one's nostrils.

I breathed deeply but no air reached my chest.

I cannot predict what will happen on this autumn morning. Will the clouds descend or remain suspended between sky and earth? This season consummates my sense of confusion, yet for some unfathomable reason I love it.

The distance from home to work is not far. I emerged from the door of my building, determined to walk. As I reached for the iron door key, my fingers touched the car key. Will it rain? I wasn't carrying an umbrella. I looked back at the sky. No change. Hard to tell. Would these clouds unload their burden of moisture on us or stay there watching?

The car key was cold. I warmed it between my fingers. When I unlocked the car door and started the motor, I felt reassured.

My anxiety began as I neared the office. I would never find a place to park. My fears were realized, and only after a long search did I find a space.

The day would be like all the others, with nothing new except tedious newspaper stories, and even this "news" was hardly new.

Visitors came and went, and I finished reading one newspaper only to pick up another. The contradictions between what was really happening in society and the reports in the papers kept growing, but my confusion didn't. It had reached an extreme years ago. Autumn's weather fluctuations only deepened the question of where reality lay. Of all the seasons, autumn is the most dear to my spirit because I realize that summer is gone and winter is coming. That alone is sufficient to make me love the depth of autumn, patient and tender as it conveys us from one sharply defined season to another.

What happened in the world to make autumn angry like summer and thundering like winter?

A downpour of rain crashed against the office windows, announcing the clouds' decision to hurl down their load. Through the window I watched people running, some soaking wet, others carrying umbrellas. But why do the ones with umbrellas run despite their protection from the rain?

The din of car horns rose from the streets where water was slowing movement and stalling engines.

A few visitors wandered into my office. Did they come to see me or were they simply seeking shelter from the sky's torrents?

The weather reports had not mentioned rain today. But why be surprised? When had we ever known what would happen to us next, in the next minute or next instant? It was past two in the afternoon and one of the visitors was still present. I felt a stifling boredom with his repetitive stories.

I asked him if he'd like me to drop him off on my way home. I emphasized the words "on my way home" and he replied that it was far and out of my way. I repeated his words: Yes, it would be out of my way. I stood up, forcing him to move as well, and he got up and left. When I heard the sound of the door shutting behind him, I hurried out before another refugee from the storm, bereft of umbrella or raincoat, came seeking shelter I would not offer.

My car stalled several times on the way to the house. The crush of traffic grew as students filled the streets waiting for rides home or searching for cars and school buses.

If it hadn't been for that tedious visitor I would have left at my normal time, before the students were let loose, and avoided the waters that now slowed my journey. There was nothing to do but wait and drive slowly. The sound of car horns deafened my ears. I rolled up the window but it quickly fogged up, making it difficult to see.

As I wiped my palm across the window I saw...I wasn't sure, it was so short a glimpse...I saw a friend, her head uncovered, walking in the rain, without umbrella, shawl or raincoat. I didn't see her feet, but they must have been immersed in water. The window fogged again and I wiped it, but my wet friend had passed from view. I looked around but could see nothing. I wiped the steam from the other window only to see waves of people going this way and that, most of them running, all of them hurrying. My friend had disappeared amidst this confusion of rain, fog and opaque glass. Had I been certain it was her hat I saw, I would have driven her home and not left her to the storm's floods and tumult.

If I had wiped the glass a few seconds earlier I would have seen her clearly. If the cars in front had moved faster, or if I had been stopped a little longer. If any number of things had happened differently, I would have called to her and invited her to come with me. But was the woman I saw really the friend I knew? It seemed to me that her hair had turned gray and her dress was untidy. The eyes of the woman I saw in the rain

# For a Pittance

# For a Pittance

In my travels I came to an unfamiliar city, to a street where there were no people, no shops, no storefronts. Why was I there? I wanted to observe the character of the city, to wander and watch. I am now a tourist. I need to be a tourist. A passing visitor. I won't stay long, I won't allow a single root to penetrate the soil of this city. I can't bother myself with tearing up roots that have escaped my watchful eye and dug into the earth. I don't want to carry any memories with me, any longings, when I leave. I'm tired of fragmented memories, disassociated yearnings, and disjointed dreams. My failed attempts to forget accumulate so that on my departure my cases carry an even heavier weight than when I first arrived.

A large group of people had gathered around the front garden and doorway of a house. I threaded my way into the crowd, not out of curiosity to know why they had gathered, but more to flee from my own soul which kept harassing me with silent unanswerable questions.

Inside the house, a number of people strolled about in a large room. Some of them conversed with companions, others were writing on notepads or paper. I watched them closely. Rather than ask them what they were doing, I walked by where they were standing or moving. I saw furniture lining the four walls, but its placement bore no resemblance to the way furniture is normally arranged in a house. Each piece bore two numbers, one indicating the sequence of placement and the other a price. So this wasn't a house, but a furniture sale.

After further wandering I realized it was not a commercial display but the estate sale of a family who was selling their household effects.

The furniture ranged from antique to a few years old. There were no new pieces. Even the carefully folded sheets, towels and curtains were clearly worn.

I saw people approaching a podium behind which sat two men who appeared to be supervising the sale. They took the tag number of the piece of furniture, received a check or cash, and handed the buyer a receipt. Then a third person would appear, walk over to where the item was displayed, and place a tag marked "sold" on it. This completed the item's role in the sale and it them became the property of new owners, in a new house, for new use. For an hour I remained there, transfixed by these proceedings. On my way out I made a final turn by the furniture and noticed that very little had been sold.

I returned to the hotel, thinking about the belongings displayed for sale, then about their owners. Why were they selling their furniture? Had they become bored with it? Were they exchanging old for new? Why I was reluctant to think that they might be in financial straits, I don't know. I think that I didn't want to consider depressing scenarios. I'm here as a tourist without connections to the past or future. Traveling places one in the present, cut off from what comes before or after, so why allow the concerns of others to preoccupy present experience? People I don't even know?

Several days later I found myself returning to the same house and standing once more among the furniture, both sold and unsold. Thinking of the sold furniture being taken to a new house and new owners depressed me, but the unsold pieces likewise stirred sorrow because they were unwanted, waiting for someone to admire them.

After another two days I went back again. Sold pieces now outnumbered unsold ones. After that, going to the house became part of my daily routine. Each time I went, there were fewer unsold items and my sorrow grew both for those that had gone and those that remained.

I hadn't thought about buying anything from the sale, but then I decided that if possible I would buy the last item remaining, the item in which no one else had showed interest.

The front gate of the house was locked when I finally went, but I felt an intense desire to go inside. I had grown accustomed to my daily visits to the house, and with each visit that familiar, oppressive yearning for a home returned, directed toward a house whose owners, history and fate I didn't know.

I had seen a part of that history through the belongings displayed for sale, but what about their owners? The people who had made the house their home, who had daily put these possessions to use? Would the house long for its former occupants and their belongings that once filled it after it had been emptied?

A flood of questions filled my mind as my hand pressed the doorbell. I was certain that no one would answer, but after a few seconds, only a few seconds, the door opened and a man's head peered out.

"Have all the furnishings been sold?" I asked.

He opened the door and invited me in. Like any young Arab woman, I was afraid to enter an unfamiliar house at a man's invitation. I repeated my question, and he asked me to wait a moment. He returned carrying a thick book with a heavy cover, and said with a scoffing smile, "This is all that's left." I asked him the price. He pointed to the corner of the cover

18

where there was a number identifying it as the last item left in the house and a tag marked with a nominal price. I quickly opened my purse and handed him the few coins required. After first turning away, I stopped and went back to thank him. I saw in his eyes and smile a profound sadness.

There was no title on the book's cover. When I opened it, I found photographs glued to the pages with care—it was a photograph album.

I clutched the book tightly, afraid that it would escape from my hands, afraid that I would lose it, even though I knew it was so heavy that it would not possibly slip or be left behind without my knowing. It was as if I was carrying a treasure. All the others bought furniture. Furniture used by those people whom I now carried under my arm. No matter what was said about them, and even if history recorded the stories of their lives, the album I carried revealed their real selves. I quickened my pace to get back to the hotel. Once there I threw myself on the bed and opened the album.

I turned the pages, sometimes quickly, sometimes slowly. It was full of photos of elderly and middle-aged men and women, young adults, teenagers and children. No names, no captions, no dates either below the pictures or on their backs. Who were all these people?

Did all of them live in that house? And how are they related?

Which ones were selling the furniture? And why? Where did all the others go, or any of them for that matter?

Countless questions gathered in my mind.

Suddenly it struck me that I had purchased this weighty past at the very time I was determined to flee from my own past. And there I was, doggedly insisting on buying the past of others!

Would I suffer with them or share their happiness? If their past had been happy, why would they have put it up for sale?

Their past is a commodity displayed for sale, and indeed, it had found a customer, but what would the buyer do with it? Why preserve it if its owners abandoned it?

I began at the first page, on which was placed a large picture that almost covered the paper. It showed a number of men and women. The older ones were sitting while the younger men and women stood behind, and children rested on the floor in the foreground.

So these three generations made up the family that had sold their past. Which one of them was responsible for selling it. Members of the older generation, if any were still alive, could not have abandoned their past. And wouldn't the middle generation want to leave this period of time to the next generation as mementos to cherish?

Such young children could not have decided such an important matter. But who am I to impose this judgment on them, for perhaps they're no longer young.

I began the onerous task of figuring out the relationships between these unknown people, and even more difficult, to ascertain their fates.

Some of the pictures were taken at weddings, children's birthdays, and award ceremonies.

The pages devoted to children began with the cradle and progressed by stages in each child's growth. Here is a child sleeping, there in someone's arms, possibly his mother's. Then he's eating with a spoon, next taking a step, perhaps his first, and so on until he goes to school. I think it must be his first day from his obvious happiness and the worry apparent on his parents' faces, knowing their son has embarked on his first journey into life's difficulties.

I grew tired of turning the pages in sequence. It only exacerbated my anxiety, so I began flipping through them haphazardly. By chance, I opened to a picture of the group sitting at a dinner table, one of the pieces that had been at the sale. I peered at the chairs and cupboard; yes they were the ones I had seen.

Now I was sure that this album belonged to the family. I had feared discovering that I had deceived myself and bought the album of a family bearing no relation to the estate sale.

Another picture showed the piano I had seen. There followed a series of children and teenage girls playing it, but no adults.

I started turning the pages again, searching for these children and teenagers. Some of the faces resembled those playing the piano, some having grown a little or a lot.

The people in a garden photo outnumbered the family members shown in the picture on the first page. The extras must be guests, and I wasn't going to bother with them; it was difficult enough to keep up with the people in the original family.

I searched for a clear series of pictures that would reveal the relationships between the members of this family who had entered my life. The day ended, midnight passed, and I was still investigating my new family whom I had bought for a pittance.

In the morning I returned to their old house carrying the heavy album. I wanted to ask the man who had sold it to me about the people in the photographs. I wanted to rest from my exploration into the lives of people and events outside the realm of my own memories.

I rang the doorbell several times. I waited, then pounded on the door but it did not wish to yield to any living person.

In this unfamiliar country, neighbors know nothing about each other, and if they did, they would not answer questions, and if they answered, they would say the matter did not concern them, really meaning that it should not concern me.

Those who had bought the home's furniture were now sitting on its chairs or sleeping in its beds or eating dinner at its table. They had brought beauty into their lives by buying a new piece of furniture for their homes. Those who had sold the furniture had some reason for doing so and now their desire had been realized. And I...I am the already burdened person who has purchased a new burden, the time, place and owners of which remain a mystery.

In my room I carried the album to the wastebasket but it was too large and wouldn't fit. I left it on the top of the basket and hurried out as if fleeing from a clinging ghost.

In the street I stared hard at people's faces, recognizing in many of them resemblances to those in the photograph album.

It was the same story in the restaurant, bookstore and theater.

When I came back to my room that night it was clean and neat as usual. The album had been placed with care on the bedside table next to the lamp.

Without switching on the lamp next to the pillow I hurried to close my eyes and sleep in a darkness devoid of even a glimmer of light.

But soon morning dawned and as I prepared to rise my eyes fell first on the album. I opened it to a page framed in black, showing people dressed in mourning gathered around a coffin bedecked in flowers.

Who in the family had died? I flipped through the pages before the funeral photograph and after it. Which face was missing after the photo of the coffin?

Death...Death...Searching for who had died. Why hadn't it occurred to me that all these new acquaintances of mine might be dead? That they may all belong to the distant past?

I was squandering the present that I had planned to enjoy. I had deliberately forgotten my own past so that it wouldn't disturb the serenity of my present, the present I had rescued from crisis in order to forget the past and distance me from the future. And now I was intentionally occupying myself with an unfamiliar time and place, with people who are strangers to me. In my imagination, I had arranged a future for their past.

21

Out of deference to the dead I set down the album, apologizing to the owners of the photographs for all the stories my imagination had told about them, for all the relationships into which my conjectures had strayed in an effort to put them all neatly in place. I had acquired their past, but who had given me the right to pursue them and impose new events on their lives?

I packed my suitcase. When I went down to the reception desk to pay my bill I handed the clerk the photograph album, saying I had found it in the room where the previous guest must have forgotten it.

On my way to the airport I felt a burden lifted from one shoulder. And yet...the other shoulder weighed heavier and heavier. The present moment had ended. The weight of the past with its memories returned to press down on me. I found it difficult to breathe. Then the future came down as well, demanding to know what lay in store for it.

The past and the future resumed their familiar arguments and mutual recriminations in my mind. And the present? The present....What if I had kept the photograph album with me, what then?...If I had kept it...would I still have my present?

# On the Waiting List

# On the Waiting List

She had thought that seats on the plane were available any time she wanted. But when she went to the reservations office, the man in charge informed her that he would have to place her name on a waiting list!

Her vacation was almost over. She had visited the city, seen its tourist sites; now she missed home. A hotel is relaxing for a few days, then a yearning for one's own room returns, one's own pillow, one's daily routines in familiar haunts...but what's the use of talking to oneself?

A line of people stood behind her, waiting for their turn to talk to the reservations clerk, and this was no time for nostalgia. The clerk was looking at her, waiting for a response. She had no choice but to acquiesce. She picked up her passport and left the office, suitcase in hand. If she didn't get a seat the next day, where would she, a stranger, go? As it was, she had to spend twenty-four hours waiting, then go to the airport with her luggage, hoping that some other passenger wouldn't turn up so she could take that seat.

What if all the passengers appeared? How long would she remain waiting? And her job back home, would they accept the excuse that she was on a waiting list?

She stared at shop windows. There was no longer anything that enticed her; new things no longer seemed new. Waiting kills all sense of surprise and joy. She had often said that travel dissolves past and future, but now she felt the oppressive weight of the present.

She recalled her house, that past she had left behind, and her longing intensified. When would the future return her to it?

She walked without direction, wandering aimlessly, unable to plan even for the next day. Perhaps it would be the end of her trip, perhaps not.

She had not paid attention to where she was going, and looked up to find herself in a residential neighborhood. Some of the houses were lit up, others were dark.

What were their occupants doing? Preparing for the evening's activities? Greeting guests? Are they happy? Tired? What's happening inside? Debates? Quarrels? Conversations? Boisterous or tranquil?

It was autumn and some of the windows were shut, their curtains drawn. Each house a world unto itself. Were people inside them waiting? Waiting for a seat on an airplane, or for something more important?

What was more important now? From her perspective, putting her mind at rest about her travel was most important. But for what were the inhabitants of these houses waiting?

She had wandered far into a new and unfamiliar part of the city. In her suitcase was a card with the name and address of her hotel. As dusk descended, all the street lights came on. How to get back? She had no idea which direction to go.

She stood waiting for a taxi, but none drove past. A large bus stopped, but she didn't know which number she needed to reach the neighborhood of her hotel. She asked the driver where he was going, and he replied that he was going near the hotel. She boarded. There were not many passengers.

People got on and off. Everyone knew which stop they wanted; she alone did not know how long her wait would be. She watched for the driver to indicate when she should get off. Her eyes fastened on his lips, but every time he announced a stop he motioned for her to wait.

Finally, he indicated she should prepare to get off at the next stop. She stood up and waited close to the door.

She stepped off the bus and studied her surroundings. There was no street sign in sight. She waited, hoping to spot someone to ask, but no one was about. She walked, not knowing whether she was heading in the right direction.

She saw a car stop, and two people got out. Before they went into the house, she raced over to ask directions, and one of them pointed to the street leading to her hotel. She walked down it, anticipating seeing the hotel's name…expecting…waiting…then suddenly she saw the familiar square, the hotel's name in lights flashing, its garden in front. Cars were stopping at the door and people getting in and out. Suitcases were arriving, others leaving.

Cars continued on their way, the glass door continued opening and closing, a routine of waiting.

People in front of her headed toward the reception desk to retrieve their keys and ask about any messages waiting for them.

She didn't inquire at the desk, for no one here knew her. If there was something sitting in the slot of her room key, she hoped it would be a letter. She decided not to sit in the reception hall where a number of other people were waiting.

A hotel employee approached, calling her name. He asked when she planned to depart. "I'm waiting," she replied

"Until when?" he asked.

When he saw the confusion and embarrassment on her face, he gently asked that she let him know when she was certain. She was about to answer that she would never be certain, but, on the verge of tears, she rushed to the elevator instead. She interpreted the employee's look to mean that he understood her situation.

She stared at the telephone in her room. She had become accustomed to its silence. How she wished it would ring now, though at home its endless ringing exasperated her.

In earlier times a camel would have been readied to take her, or a horse, carriage, or car. But now…that cursed machine, the airplane with its fixed dates, seats, destinations and departure times, stood in her way. They say the world has advanced, been modernized, its distances shortened, with no place too far. But that vacant seat on the plane, isn't it distant? Will the wait for it be short or long?

Her hotel room contained neither television nor radio. Should she go to the lounge to watch the evening's television programs, and be stared at by other patrons as if she was a serpent whose head needed to be struck and crushed?

Yesterday, she had gone to the lounge, thinking it was her last night. She sat watching television programs the entire evening. The children's shows! They made her feel old. The news? Full of natural and human disasters. The serial? She had no idea what had happened before and she wouldn't be here to see what came next…A moment in time disconnected from what preceded it and what would follow, so why bother watching? Then there was the Indian film, in which the actors had drenched their hair with so much oil she could almost smell it, reminiscent of fried fish.

So here was an entire day she must remain on the waiting list.

She picked up the newspaper and magazine she had read earlier that morning. She had already perused the world news and the political editorials. Now she would wade through all the sections whether she enjoyed them or not. She must pass the time, willingly or otherwise.

A page of classified advertisements. Ads announcing houses for rent and others for sale. She looked over the details for each house. Nothing in them suited her. Some were too big, others too small, still others she just didn't like. Why not?

She read the employment section. She wasn't qualified to be a truck driver or master chef or electrician. She found no position appropriate for her. What if she had to remain here, buy a house and find work to make ends meet?

The horoscope page? She had never given any thought to the sign under which her birthday fell. She read all the predictions, picked the one that pleased her, and made it her sign, thus finding a future that appealed to her.

She glanced at the crossword puzzle, uncertain if crossing, intersecting and mixing words to solve the puzzle would dissolve the tension of waiting, or if it would be better to leave it as is.

On the page with letters from people seeking advice about affairs of the heart, she read about a sixteen year old girl who loved a neighbor boy two years her senior. He shares this deep love but is not yet able to marry and wants her to wait. Her family refuses to allow her to wait. This was a summary of the problem as the girl explained it, and she ended with a plea to the love doctor not to recommend that she give up his love or break off the relationship. So what was she to do?

Another heartsick soul, bewildered and seeking guidance, was in love with a colleague at work, and waited for him to fulfill his pledge made many years earlier to marry her. She was now over thirty, and he still asked her to wait until he could convince his aging parents who depended on his care. She had no option but to wait, for everyone knew of her attachment to him. Besides, who would propose marriage to a woman her age who was known to be already involved with her colleague?

A third letter concluded the section. The man whom this woman loved and had waited for had married someone else. The one whom she thought had asked her to wait no longer waited for her; he disappeared from her list, which contained no one else. She had waited years and he had broken his promise, so how could she restore in herself a willingness to wait? Now she despaired, for she could not wait again for a new man to marry her.

She threw down the magazine. She had no wish to deal with other people who were waiting, nor did she believe that waiting required two sides. If one side gave up, then the other might still be willing to wait.

In her baggage was a novel she had not yet finished. She returned to it, but when she reached the last chapter, she suddenly felt afraid. After she finished the novel, then what? What next?

The wait, the anticipation! What were the other people doing whose names were on the same list? Or those who weren't on the list?

Or those whose travel plans were assured? Weren't they all waiting the end of their travels?

This newspaper which she had already read! How many people were waiting for the morning to read it again?

The classified advertisements! How many fates depended on those ads? Sellers of houses and buyers of houses...weren't they waiting?

The job vacancies. So many were hanging their hopes on them, anticipating an announcement, an interview and then the first day of work.

The horoscope. Many believed it, waiting for what the future brings.

Every newspaper and magazine contained a crossword puzzle, so there must be countless people anticipating the pleasure of solving it.

The letters of the lovelorn and the television programs, and on, and on. Waiting...expecting...However long this moment persists, it will pass, but waiting for the next moment is still waiting.

And after this long empty night, then what? What? What then?

The next day she was on the airplane. She slumped into her seat. The flight attendant offered a platter of sweets, just the kind she liked. She relished them. When she felt airsick, the attendants made a fuss over her. Was there anyone back home who would show such concern for her?

A tray of food came and they asked her what she would like to drink. Just like that: she was asked, she answered, and the drink appeared.

Next to her was a bell. One touch if she needed anything...She slid her fingers over it then withdrew them. What did she want?

She closed her eyes and relaxed. When she opened them again, the tray had been taken away.

A perfume cart stood beside her. The attendant bent down to ask her what perfume she preferred, for a price that was duty free.

It was as if she sat on a throne. Food and drink came to her. At the touch of a bell her requests were met. The attendants even demonstrated how to use the life jacket in case the plane encountered any trouble, so concerned were they for her safety!

In a few hours she would return to her house, the house she loved, the house for which she had been pining. She would open the suitcases, hang up the clothes and straighten her room.

She'd leap from the bed in the morning and rush to work. Heavy traffic might make her late to the office and make her nervous twitch worse. What would be waiting for her at the office?

She was accustomed to this morning anxiety, and her evening worries had been with her ever since she had begun to remember. Yet she was afraid to forget, to not remember.

After this restful time on the airplane, for which she had waited and worried about the uncertainty of waiting, she would return home, return to the familiar details, the familiar worry, the anxiety and tension she knew so well.

There she would not have to wait. Her life there was on a track, she couldn't change its direction. Her familiar daily routine would propel her, like a blindfolded ox walking round and round the water wheel. (The ox never realizes that he trudges only in circles.)

Her eyes were unfettered, seeing, knowing, understanding. But they would not have to wait any more.

She closed them again and imagined herself there, somewhere, waiting.

Papers From an Ancient Archive

# Papers from an Ancient Archive

She's moving to a new house! The dream of a lifetime realized. A new house in a neighborhood she loves. As they looked over the many pieces of furniture, her guests warned: packing all these belongings is going to wear you down! And moving them to a new house will be exhausting.

She didn't need their advice. She knew that she would tire and that it would take her long hours of work to prepare for this event for which she had waited so long.

But this time the wait would not be in vain, her dreams were coming true! But were they really, she wondered? How long had she dreamed of changing houses? So many years had passed she couldn't count them, and she asked herself was it possible to measure dreams in length and breadth?

The large obvious items would not be a problem. But the small pieces which she must securely wrap so they wouldn't be crushed, these were going to be tiresome.

Before she began to pack, she decided to get rid of the things she no longer needed.

She brought down some old suitcases from the attic.

She opened the first one, and the odor of mothballs permeated the room. Extra winter clothing. She held up one piece and turned it around, but neither the color nor design appealed to her, and, she discovered, it no longer fit. Her body had changed, her tastes had changed, or something else she didn't recognize had changed. In any event, the clothes no longer suited her. She shut the case again. She would give it to the wife of the doorman.

The second case held summer clothes smelling of mildew. She placed it beside the winter case.

The third case was filled with papers. Piles of papers, some handwritten, others typed, intermingled with newspapers and magazines.

No doubt she had set them aside long ago because they had some significance to her, but why had she saved them all these years?

Her curiosity impelled her to open one of the magazines. As she turned the pages, an envelope with her name and address fell out. Her name and address? That was her address over a quarter century ago.

As she flipped through the pages, more envelopes fell out, all bearing her name, although the address varied.

A quarter of a century ago. Twenty years ago! Ten years! Fifteen!

The address changed many times, as did the names of cities and places of work and even "temporary" addresses. But when had her address ever been permanent? And during which period was it "temporary"?

Pages of letters with no envelopes. Where had she been living when these letters arrived?

She began to read the letters, starting from the end, with the signature and the author. The vault of the past began to open before her eyes. Mountains of letters from different countries. But what about the authors? Some were still living, some had died, others she wasn't sure, and about one she could no longer remember anything at all.

She knew she had received a large number of letters, but hadn't realized that she had kept so many of them. Why had she preserved them? Had they once held some meaning for her? She saw in some a past she no longer remembered, yet she could recall other events not mentioned in the letters. She entered this vault, closing the door behind her. She put on her glasses.

One letter read: "You called my love for you an insult, but I called it God." The date on it was more than a quarter of a century old. When had she spoken these words? She knew that she had never written such a letter to anyone. At the time the letter was written she was so timid she never wrote to strangers, so where had this dialogue taken place? Had he heard it from someone? Had she said that love was an insult, and he said it was God?

A thick piece of paper, the program from her university graduation ceremony. She read the list of names. Where were these fellow students now?

A photograph fell out from between the papers. The students of her class, all male, everyone present except her. No, she did not talk to men in those days. Virtuous girls didn't talk to boys, so how could she have had her picture taken with them?

She wondered if they had kept copies of the picture. She had kept it...yet not really, for, had she not exhumed this vault of the past, she would never have found it.

She dug deeper.

A letter said: "Hurry and read the second chapter of my novel; I've already begun the third, but you know that I can't publish it without first getting your opinion, and the due date is approaching."

The letters fell out one after anther. One said: "I will continue to write you despite your silence and the torture of waiting for a reply."

Yes, he had waited a long time, and would wait until death.

A number of letters remained in their envelopes. All of them were in the same handwriting, but the addresses changed. This made it easy for her to collect them letters together.

The enveloped piled up. She slid the paper out of each one and began to read. Why hadn't she responded to them?

She glanced again at the dates. The missives spanned ten years, each one imploring, waiting. Why had these letters persisted in waiting for a response even though she never wrote?

The letters were lengthy, full of their author's feelings. Had she wanted, by not responding, to cut off hope so that they would stop? Or did she agonize over this boiling passion, and wanted to pretend she was above it, thus making it stop.

A letter read: "Don't be disturbed by London. You'll get used to it. Like you, I felt a sense of alienation at first, but now I'm filled with longing for its perpetually green gardens."

Another said: "It's amazing how much you love Britain! What is it that draws you to it? I haven't spoken to anyone since I arrived, the English are so harsh and haughty. Britain is no longer great, so how can the people think they are superior to us?"

It seemed that the next letter came from the same person, for it read: "After a long silence, I have finally spoken with someone, but it was a person from Brazil who is in my college, and who, like me, hates Britain. So tell me, do you still yearn for this place?"

Yearn? Yearn? She remembered how she returned to London after an absence of ten years and encountered a country she no longer knew. She remembered saying, "I went to the country I loved, yearning for it, and was cured of my love."

A letter said: "Our town waits for you always and loves you as much as you love it. We expected your arrival on Saturday, the 14th of last month, though I knew snow was falling and the road was closed. But I thought, perhaps she'll find a plane. When the sun began to sink and finally set, I despaired and went to visit some friends, leaving their telephone number with my family just in case."

But he hadn't really despaired because he said, "I left the telephone number with my family." The year wasn't given, nor even which month. Her return to that town was happy anyway, so why search for the date?

The season wasn't winter now, and snow didn't block the roads; still she couldn't travel to that town, for although the roads leading to it were open, her heart was closed.

Another letter said: "Forgive me for not responding sooner, but I was still searching for the book you requested. When I find it, I'll send it immediately."

The signature was illegible, there was no envelope, and the first page was missing. From where had it come? Who had written it? What book had she requested, and did this person eventually send it?

She searched among the letters for another one in similar handwriting, but with no success.

A single orphaned letter. For all she knew she might have stolen someone else's letters. Had she, she wondered?

A letter said: "The desert is vast. My eyes move from horizon to horizon. Perhaps it has improved my eyesight. Your Beirut is a jungle of stone; it constrained my ability to see. When are you going to quit that bizarre city?"

The letter was ten years old. True, Beirut was a strange city. A jungle of stone, the writer called it. What would he call it now that it had become a jungle of guns?

A letter said: "Don't say you've despaired of life. For you haven't really. You love life very much, you want to live in the fullest sense of the word. But pretending to be sad is part of growing up. Like you, I wanted to proclaim a sadness that really wasn't there. Then true despair entered my life. Don't be like me." Yes, after some twenty years true despair had come to her, and her desires were scattered in a thousand and one directions.

A letter said: "Why don't you improve your handwriting? Deciphering these scribbles exhausts me. When I write I purposely make my words clear so they're easy to read." If her handwriting wasn't clear then, fifteen years ago, what would they say if they saw it now? It had become even more inscrutable as her haste in writing increased. She accelerated time lest more escape than had already passed her by.

A picture of a friend was inscribed, "In memory of a beautiful distant past." The inscription was thirty years old. Was there really a past then? Was it distant? And beautiful? What would her friend say if she was inscribing a photograph today?

A small notebook with yellowed paper. The paper was on the verge of crumbling. She turned several pages, and saw her handwriting on them. It was better than now.

On the right side of the page were numbers, and in front of them were quotes attributed to authors—verses of poetry, proverbs, and quotations from poets, writers, thinkers and public figures. Next to each were remarks identified as her own (me) or those of the speaker. The verses, proverbs and quotations all talked about the past, so did the words signed *me*.

1 - I love the bloom of the narcissus because it reminds me of a past that has not yet arrived. me
2 - In desire I turned back, but as I turned, the spring of life receded; can desire bring back the spring? (Ali Mahmoud Taha)
3 - The past is an oil painting that appears beautiful the further you move away from it. (Oscar Wilde)

She had placed herself with Ali Mahmoud Taha and Oscar Wilde and other famous writers. The past...the past...She remembered how she had saved clippings and other things, thinking she would cherish them when they had become a part of the past. And now...Now she was deliberately working to eradicate the past. She wondered whether she consumed the past before it arrived, so that when it did come it was already over?

A letter said: "I wish you could be with me, so that I wouldn't feel the gloom that comes with sunset."

What is the gloom of a tomb like? What is it like? What?

Whenever they asked her, "When shall we see you?" she would answer "Let's leave it to chance." But that chance never came. She had intentionally tried to foil it, not realizing that death was to be the final barrier between them and the promise for which they would wait, the promise that would never come.

She pushed away the papers. A mountain of papers. Masses of papers. All her papers. She had decided to eradicate the past. So why had it returned to her? Why? She must shut this vault and firmly lock its bolt.

Masses of letters lay in front of her...She abandoned them and fled to an adjoining room. On the television Umm Kulthum was singing. The performance was nearing its end, the audience was applauding and cheering and shouting, and Umm Kulthum was standing singing: "I see you holding back tears, patience is your virtue, but how is it that love has no power over you?" Then Umm Kulthum stepped back and the curtains fell and quietly closed in front of the stage and musicians. The cheering and applause grew louder, the curtains remained closed, the applause and cheering went on and on, until the din finally died down. The audience turned from the stage and began to leave the hall. The curtains descended completely. The announcer said, "And so ends tonight's concert..."

An old archival film was presented and ended. She heard herself finishing the song: "Yes, I'm longing and lovesick but it is not I who reveal such secrets."

The Beirut newscast was talking about a violation of the new cease-fire.

*Wag Wag Airport*

# Waq Waq Airport

My friend and I were waiting for our plane to leave. The noise in the hall prevented us from clearly hearing the announcements of the flight arrival and departure and the gate number for boarding. Piles of personal effects, parcels and large handbags surrounded a group of nearby travellers. They wore several coats and cloaks, one on top of the other. As I stared at them, my friend commented, "They must be going to some country with a cold climate." It was late spring, but the heat had come early, rendering the air conditioning ineffective, though its hum grew louder as it reverberated through the loudspeakers of the public address system.

I was about to respond that these travellers were not going sightseeing, they were returning to their country, either temporarily or for good. Their economic circumstances obviously did not permit them to ship their belongings, so they were wearing what they could, and carrying the rest by hand. In this way, their checked baggage would meet the airline's weight limits.

Between the words she spoke and the words I hadn't spoken came an announcement for some plane either about to take off or land, I couldn't hear which.

I looked at my friend for clarification, but she shook her head. She hadn't heard clearly either. I got up and asked one of the travellers his destination, and he named a place with which I had no connection. I moved to a woman traveller and asked her the same question, and then asked another, and another, but heard only the same answer. I searched in vain for someone flying in the same direction we wanted to go.

My anxiety began to mount. The boarding pass didn't mention the gate number for our departure, and I couldn't spot a stewardess or steward to help me. Suddenly, I saw the group with all the bags and coats hurrying toward one of the departure gates. They seemed in pain as they carried on their shoulders and dragged by hand their loads of belongings, together with their children who were almost crushed under the feet of those rushing for the gate. But their families dragged them along firmly as they ran, each wanting to get to the gate before the other. The children began to scream.

At that moment I heard a voice with an authoritative tone yelling, "Stand in single file...Stop trying to push ahead, you'll all get on, each in your turn." The clamor rose as those rushing to the gate heard what was happening, and they ran even harder, pushing and shoving to get to the front. The bags got mixed up with each other, and people started yelling to others to drag along pieces left behind. These requests were carried out, or a stream of curses issued forth, for no one was able to carry an extra bag, or even drag it. More children were crying; their calls for help grew louder as they lost sight of their families.

Finally all the passengers stood by the gate ready for the flight, sweat dripping down their faces. Some of them licked at it with their tongues, others wiped it with their shoulder or on the shoulder of the person in front of them. The shoulder used in this way whipped around and struck any face close by....The struck face screamed in turn that it was not to blame....Cries of exasperation rose again, trying to reduce the heat and sweat. Children threw themselves down, rolling on the ground, calling for their families who were virtually hidden behind their bags.

The loudspeaker announced in a loud and very clear voice: "The gate at which you are waiting is not your departure gate. Your gate is..."

The crowd spun around and once again tried to push ahead. Their movement was blocked by waiting bags, children sprawled on the ground and women sitting clasping their belongings with infants sleeping on top.

I stood there staring in distress at them until the last traveller, who had been the first in line at the wrong gate, had left.

I turned my head looking for the new gate. It lay in the completely opposite direction. My eyes focused on the back of the last person standing in the waiting line.

He glanced back as he dragged along his belongings, wife and children, handed over his boarding card, and disappeared through the gate.

This troop had hardly vacated the departure hall when the airport personnel burst out laughing, wiping away tears from laughing so hard. Although I didn't understand all their words, I hear clearly what they were saying.

They were exchanging congratulations for this scene which they had both authored and staged.

I had almost forgotten everything around me save for this tragic drama the authors, producers and other spectators of which considered a comedy.

My friend was standing some distance away, her gaze moving in amazement between the two gates where this drama had been staged.

I approached her. "Is this life?" she was muttering. "Tragedy turns into comedy and comedy to tragedy?" I don't think she heard me when I said, "What saddens me is that the one who was fastest and most

48

energetic became last in line, and the winner was the one who didn't make much effort."

But I don't know if she heard me because she then said, "Everyone knew what was going to happen except the actors themselves."

"So they were spared the trouble of memorizing their roles," I replied.

"And the role of prompter was eliminated," she said.

"No," I said, "he was there to prompt the witnesses."

The public address system announced the last call for passengers travelling to…from gate…

"After that scene," my friend said, "I'm thinking of changing my mind and not going anywhere."

A stewardess approached, calling our names. I said to my friend, "Give her the boarding pass before they leave us and the plane takes off."

"And before respect and politeness disappear…Can you guarantee that they won't?"

"I don't know, but how could they disapear?" I asked.

"They're dying, dying!" she exclaimed. "Haven't you heard of anything called death?"

The stewardess smiled as she helped us board the bus.…On the steps of the plane, a steward and stewardess welcomed us and led us to our seats. "Try to forget that scene and savor this politeness and respect," my friend advised.

"Yes," I interrupted. "Yes, I'll try before death takes it by surprise."

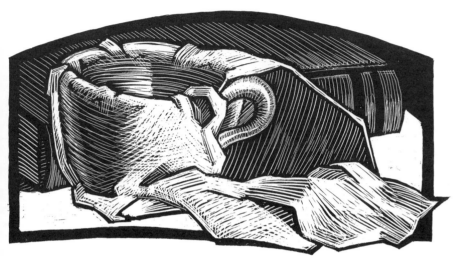

Fires of the Past

# Fires of the Past

Workers filled the house, wrapping furniture, kitchen appliances and glassware. Everything in the house was being readied for the move. These things would go ahead, so she could be assured of their safety.

Preparations for moving! How many times had she prepared to move, yet how she needed stability.

When friends would ask her why she wasn't satisfied with an annual vacation, she was surprised. Why travel just to stay in a hotel, when all she ever wanted was to have her own house? But houses...houses didn't understand her simple need: to have a home in which she could truly settle.

Yet she had never stayed in one house, and settling had not been part of her life.

This time she had thought that stability had finally arrived. She had been twenty-seven years in one place. Even though she had moved from house to house, they had all been within the same city at least, and she was independent, not subservient to anyone. A woman who made her own decisions. Long ago she had decided to stay here where she knew people and people knew her, where acquaintances matured into friendships, becoming almost like the family she had always lacked. A family without blood ties.

"Is all the furniture in the middle room ready to be packed?" a worker asks.

"Yes," she answered with thinking.

She suddenly stood up, unable to remember what was in the middle room. The glass and chinaware she had collected over a lifetime. They could never survive the move. They must remain here. "And what will we do with the books lining the shelves?" they asked her.

"Put them in the room set aside for the things staying here," she replies without hesitation.

These books were the rewards of a lifetime of study and friendship, all gathered together in one place. Yet here she was ordering them to be dispersed with the wave of a finger.

She stopped in front of the bookshelves trying to read, but her eyesight was failing. She put on her glasses.

A collection of important books. Important because most of them contained inscriptions to her. Affectionate, lovely, moving inscriptions, with the authors' signatures below. On the shelves of this library she has gathered the signatures of the most famous writers in the Arab world. What to do with them? Take them with her? She would need a special truck just for the books. And if she did take them, how could she get them into her new country? It would require permission, and they might be confiscated in customs before being allowed in, if they were allowed to enter at all.

These precious volumes must remain here. Keeping them secure was preferable to moving and torturing books accustomed to respect.

Out of sight in a safe is a bag filled with papers—letters, notebooks, personal notes. These, too, have to stay, she could never move them. Such a quantity of papers could never pass the customs inspector's eyes unnoticed.

Her friends who penned these papers…would they approve (or have approved) of strangers reading their thoughts and feelings, when she had been so sparing with them herself, only taking them out to study on rare occasion? Reading their words awakened sorrows and passions from the past. What if strangers read them and carelessly damaged them, ignorant of their historic, literary and human value? No, a thousand and one no's!

"Leave them here," she signalled with an outstretched hand, although she doesn't know what the word "here" signifies. "Here" will no longer be here.

Nonetheless, keeping them here is better than exposing them to fire, damage and negligence.

Her possessions stay while she departs to a new home. Finally, moving to another house Another house! A new house? Hadn't she tired of new houses and wishing they would become old?

But what good would it do to admit to exhaustion?

The truck arrived to take her household belongings, car and clothes. She stood on the balcony overlooking the sea. In her new country, her apartment will look over a river. And what of it? As long as she can see water flowing before her, what do its sources or destination matter?

She couldn't bear to say goodbye to her possessions, to check that they were all there, or even see them, unrecognizable in cartons and masses of packing paper. She ran downstairs to the street, abandoning the workers to do as they please with the house and her belongings, to move or leave whatever they chose.

When she returned the house was empty.

She walked into the room set aside for the things staying behind. There were piles upon piles of belongings, and she could almost hear the room complain of this abuse. It was accustomed to being pampered and ordered, with a special place and arrangement for everything.

She walked out of the room and hurried to where she left her suitcases. These suitcases would be her companions on the journey. Her eyes filled with tears. Would this companionship bring joy or sorrow?

At the airport, the full significance of leaving finally struck her. She had to remind herself that she was going to a land where there were friends, family, warmth and safety.

Her sister and a mutual friend greeted her in Baghdad. They looked exhausted, having spent the entire night waiting after her plane's departure from Larnaca was delayed a full ten hours. She felt embarrassed by the trouble she had caused them, but they welcomed her with affection, and it was affection that she needed, especially at this moment.

In the morning, she began her new work. She visited her director, who received her graciously, and she met her new colleagues.

I will get used to their warmth, she thought. I need new friends, having left behind friendships matured over a lifetime.

As she arranged her new apartment, the beloved home she had given up never strayed from her thoughts.

How many houses had she lived in during her life? Would this be the last one, or only temporary like all the ones before?

Several days later, as she opened the new door, a large envelope bearing stamps of the country she had left fell from where it had been lodged. She hurried to her room, unable to read. She put on her glasses. In the envelope were cuttings from newspapers with notices of receptions held in honor of her final farewell to the country. Final...final? Then everything was finished...Everything?

No, it wasn't all over. Her beloved books were still there. The inscriptions from friends with their signatures. Her personal mementos. Her most valuable possessions. Consciously or not, she had left behind the things of most significance for her.

Why had she done that? Why? Were these things able to travel to her on their own? And she...can she travel to them? Visit them? See them? Bring them back? She must forget that place and all it contains...Her memories sadden her, and she needs to seek happiness.

She had never known loneliness before, but she felt it now. Entering the apartment was like walking into a hotel room. She had never enjoyed vacations because she feared the feeling of staying in a hotel. Now, in her final residence, she sits in an apartment enclosed by walls she doesn't know and which don't know her.

In the elevator she tried to be friendly. She greeted a woman but the response was cool. A man turned his face away without saying anything at all.

Loneliness is real and enduring. Yet she would get used to it. How often had she adjusted to more difficult situations than this? Did she spend her life adjusting in order to forget, and forgetting in order to adjust? But she's human. She tires and yearns, waits and wishes and feels bereft. But whom could she say that to? To whom could she talk? To whom?

There was nothing to do but wait. While she waited, travellers arrived from her former country…Neighbors from the building where she had lived and rented a room assured her that her possessions are safe.

The visitors brought gifts and letters, and reassured her that the missile that smashed into her room had not completely exploded. The new occupants of the house held her in such esteem that they rushed to extinguish the flames with large quantities of water, preventing the fire from spreading.

She remembered the words of the inscriptions in her books, the letters and personal papers. She recalled some of the phrases and their authors. She thought of the fine, invaluable tokens of friendship left behind, and she feared that they had been moved or damaged. She remembered all the furniture she left in that room. She was only allowed to bring in enough furniture for one person. For one person, and her life in that house had spanned more than a quarter of a century!

She clapped her hands over her ears so she could not hear the rush of water quenching the flames.

She shut her eyes so she couldn't see the room filled with her belongings. She wanted to forget, to close the vault of the past, the vault she opened only to savor memories she kept otherwise concealed.

She must close that room. Lock it once and for all with a key. Her hand reached into her pocket. The key wasn't there. In her suitcase, in the box of keys, in her dresser…in…

She remembered. She had left the key there…in the room flooded with water to smother the flames.

## The Doctor's Prescription

# The Doctor's Prescription

She asked the pharmacist for some tranquilizers, and he wanted to know whether she had a doctor's prescription. The question surprised her, since she wasn't requesting sleeping pills. He understood her request, he replied, but a prescription was also necessary for tranquilizers.

She pleaded with him: the tranquilizers could do no harm, she said and she had gotten used to them. He responded that it wasn't a question of what she was used to, there were dangers involved.

"Do you mean suicide?" she interrupted.

"Not exactly," he replied, "but there are dangers."

She asked him what types of tranquilizers he had in stock. He said he had only one kind and mentioned its name. It was a tranquilizer with a very limited effect, perhaps not even enough to help calm her hypertension, yet he worried that people might use it to kill themselves?

Do you realize, she asked, that if someone wanted to commit suicide with this tranquilizer, he would have to swallow hundreds of pills. That means dozens of bottles. It would take hours to swallow them, and an enormous amount of water. All that liquid would upset the stomach, and the long time needed to take the pills would provide an opportunity to reconsider the death wish. The person would have to be determined in this matter, since the pills would require even more time to take effect, and while that was happening the person might begin to despair of rushing too quickly to depart this life. One could go out like this any time, but one wouldn't be able to bring back life. Thinking over the reasons that compelled attempting suicide, one would see that they weren't as important as thought, and one might consider another chance and seeing if one could cope with the problems.

As this person began to feel drowsy, the instinct for self-preservation would take hold and she would think that she'd made a mistake, that life is more powerful. She'd try to call for help and drag herself to the nearest window or door to shout, so people would hear...One would open her eyes in the hospital, stomach having been pumped, an intravenous feeder attached to an arm, and friends all around. One would repent, and life would seem beautiful after nearly being lost.

So you see, such mild tranquilizers are hardly appropriate for suicide.

"With an intelligent woman like yourself," the pharmacist says, "who thinks through all these stages, I suppose there's no concern about..."

"About any of the dangers you're thinking about," she answered. He gave her one bottle of pills. She thanked him and left.

*    *    *    *

At the second pharmacy she needed to repeat the story.

At the third pharmacy she was given a bottle before finishing the story.

At the fourth, a few sentences sufficed, and so on at the fifth, sixth and all the others.

The newspapers reported that a woman was found dead in her bed. On the table next to her were a number of empty sleeping pill bottles and a note. "I came into this life without anyone consulting me," the note read, "but life never understood me, so I've decided to end it after sufficiently convincing myself that I can no longer endure this lack of understanding between us. This decision to end my life is mine alone."

As people read the news and looked at the smiling face in the photograph they shook their heads in sorrow. "Poor thing. She killed herself in a moment of despair," said some. "It seems that the one she loved wasn't faithful to her," said others. Psychiatrists contended that she was in full control of her senses when she made the decision to commit suicide. The pharmacists, after recognizing her picture in the papers, told no one of her conversations with them.

"We all tried to help her," her mother kept repeating between tears.

She did not take her secret with her, and yet no one said, "How much she loved life!"

*Weeping*

# Weeping

I woke one night to the sound of weeping. I looked about, then remembered there was no one else in the house. The window was open. I walked over to it, thinking that the weeping was coming from one of the neighboring houses. But it was more distant.

I went back to bed wondering who was weeping on this dark night, and what made them cry.

With great difficulty and after a long wait I fell asleep again. When I woke in the morning, I immediately remembered the nocturnal weeping, but it had ceased.

The next night the winds grew blustery. I shut the windows but the heat forced me to open them again. Had what I heard been a human wail or just the howl of the wind?

The storm continued for three nights in a row. The wind whistled and rattled against the window panes, keeping me awake. When the storm finally abated, I fell into a deep slumber after the sleeplessness of the previous nights.

Shortly before dawn I awoke to the sound of weeping again, louder and even more mournful in tone.

If only I knew who was crying! And why they were grieving so? If only I could do something to alleviate this pain!

I leaned my head out of the window. Certainly this was a woman's cry. How could this grieving woman weep so long and loudly without anyone coming to her aid? Did she choose the night to reveal her sorrow so that no eyes would see her?

Should I ask the neighbors whether they had heard the cry? But such a question might expose the secret of this unknown woman.

Several nights passed and the weeping continued. When it grew into a howling dirge I could no longer remain silent. I asked one of my neighbors if she had been able to sleep the previous nights.

"With that wind how could anyone get any decent sleep?," she replied.

So I wasn't hallucinating; I'm all right. I had begun to think that it was the constant ringing in my ears becoming louder and sharper. The doctor had told me in no uncertain terms that this condition was the result of severe mental exhaustion experienced by people with fragile nerves who don't reveal their worries. I knew full well that I was one of those people for I had undergone a myriad of laboratory and hospital examinations, x-rays, and prescriptions.

My neighbor passed on my inquiry to others, and I received several responses. But the strange thing was the most of those who heard the sound said it sounded like disjointed bursts of laughter coming from far, far away. I listened closely at night but I heard crying, and after a few nights, wailing, and finally I began to hear cries for help.

Yet whenever I looked out of the window I saw nothing but the black night, a blackness which intensified the deep reverberations in my ears of these wailing cries for help. And they say after all this that they hear laughter! I put cotton in my ears, but muffled cries, wails, howls and calls for help still reached me.

In the morning, I decided to go out to see the sunlight and perhaps forget the darkness and weeping of the night.

I wandered in streets crowded with people. No tears were coursing down cheeks, eyes sparkled with pleasure, children chirped happily.

I began to fear the coming of night, to dread the anonymous weeping and distant wails.

In one of my daylight excursions, I left the streets of the central city to stroll in a suburban district. There I noticed that a recent plantation of trees was close to reaching the goal set by the city's reforestation project. The project, which called for planting a thick belt of trees around the city, had been suggested to the city council by an environmental expert as a means to mitigate the impact of heat and aridity.

At the time the decision was made, no one realized how long it would take for the trees to grow and complete the proposed belt of woodland. Nor did it occur to us that science doesn't wait, science acts.

So it was that huge trucks came carrying tall, full-grown trees, complete with roots embedded in soil, to be set in deep gaping holes specially prepared for this purpose. The process amazed us. In the beginning, we used to visit the newly planted areas to look at the poplars lined up around us. Later, we grew accustomed to seeing the trucks bringing this balm to our city's summer heat and drought.

I roamed through the forest, awed by the power of science to move these lofty trees with thick trunks and make them seem as if they had sprung here naturally from seed. The sight of the lovely forest with its verdant green and shadows soothed me.

I returned home thinking I should visit the forest more often to calm my nerves.

That night the weeping and wailing and cries for help came again, obliterating the daylight's tranquillity.

The next morning I returned to the forest, knowing it was the cure I needed. My excursions there soon became a part of daily routine, while the weeping remained a nightly ritual. Slowly the wailing began to grow dimmer and more distant. Its sharpness continued to diminish as I increased my visits to the forest, which I believed to be the cause of my new sense of calm. It was strange, however, that the others still heard the laughter and continued to ask where it was coming from.

The poplar trees stood strong and steadfast in the path of dust storms, buffering their severity and cleansing the air. More and more of the migratory trees arrived in our city to take up residence, finding rest for themselves and providing comfort for us.

One day as I was strolling through the forest, I raised my head to see branches extending above me, tall and upright. Suddenly I bumped into the trunk of a tree. It was not upright like the others, but leaned heavily to one side. On my next visit I made straight for this tree. Its trunk inclined even more so that its branches almost touched the ground. I began to visit it regularly, witnessing its transformation, leaves getting smaller, branches thinning, until it no longer resembled its companion poplars.

I asked people about it and they replied that it was sick and might die. But I was sure that it wasn't the case, for why would its leaves still be green?

I took friends with me, and they said this phenomenon required specialists to explain. Foresters confirmed that poplars had certain qualities and characteristics not found in my tree, but they couldn't find any scientific explanation for what was happening.

The weeping and wailing and lamentations and cries for help continued but in a weak, tired whisper.

Some days passed before I visited the tree again. When I did, I found it was touching the earth. Its bend had quickly become so severe that it lay nearly flat on the ground. The leaves had become smaller and turned yellow, and the branches had grown even more thin and emaciated. Finally the tree lay down to sleep once and for all, its leaves falling around. Sand began to cover the fallen tree, no wind stirred it, and the white trunk turned black.

When I saw insects boring into its trunk I realized the tree had died. Only then did I recall a remark I had made earlier. Amidst the wonder at the power of science to uproot these trees from somewhere else and bring them to us, I had asked, "What if the trees don't want to move!" Everyone laughed, thinking I was joking.

I told my friends that the weeping willow had killed herself after dropping to her knees, imploring the earth for water but not finding the river that had once quenched her thirst. I don't think any of them understood the meaning of my words.

That night I didn't sleep, even though I heard neither weeping nor wailing, neither lamentations nor cries for help.

It was I who wept, without wailing or lamenting or calling for help...and no one heard.

# A Crutch in the Head

He said: You don't understand me.
She said: Yes, I don't understand you.
He said: I'm trying to get closer to you.
She said: And I'm becoming more distant.
He said: You admit it?

She said: You're trying to get closer to me.
He said: And you're becoming more distant.
She said: And I'm becoming more distant.
He said: You're not with me.
She said: I'm far away from you.

He said: Where are you?
She said: I'm not here.
He said: You admit it?
She said: Because I'm not with you.
He said: You don't respect my opinions!
She said: I don't respect your opinions.

He said: You admit it?
She said: My opinions differ.
He said: You'll regret it.
She said: I'll be happy.
He said: You admit it?
She said: Happiness is a need.
He said: I will never wish you happiness.

She said: I know that.
He said: Why do you oppose me?
She said: Because you want me to.
He said: Your thoughts are strange.
She said: Yes they are strange.
He said: You admit it?

She said: What do you think about changing a spare part?
He said: In the car?
She said: No.
He said: In what then?

She said: In the machine in your mind.
He said: There's no machine in my mind.

She said: What did you put in your mind today?
He said: This provocation will gain you nothing.
She said: Yes, it won't gain me anything.
He said: You admit it?
She said: I obey your wishes.
He said: Since when have you rushed to obey my wishes?
She said: Since I realized that's what you want.
He said: You admit it?
She said: When I began to understand it.
He said: What did you understand?
She said: I understood what you think about.
He said: I don't believe you understand what I think about.
She said: Yes, I don't understand what you think about.
He said: You admit it?

She said: This is what you wish.
He said: Why are you trying to keep the peace today?
She said: I'm tired of understanding.
He said: So then you understand my wishes?
She said: Let's say I understand them.
He said: But you agree that you don't understand me.
She said: Yes, I don't understand you.

He said: So you're back to your declaration that you don't understand me.
She said: I declare it so.
He said: You admit it?

She said: You want me to say that.
He said: You're feigning submission.
She said: Yes.
He said: You admit it?
She said: That's what you wish.

He said: I'm ending this discussion.
She said: Yes, your head is pounding.
He said: You admit it?
She said: What shall I say? What?

He said: Anything! Say anything that contradicts my opinion.
She said: You always wanted me to be your student. You demanded that I repeat the proverb, "He who teaches me letters, I shall be his slave."

He said: Do you admit that I'm your teacher and you're my pupil?
She said: You were my teacher and I was your pupil. But...
He said: Who's your teacher now then? Who?
She said: I thought that pretending to be your slave would make you happy, but I hurt myself, so I decided not to complete my studies.

He said: You call the house a school?
She said: You're beginning to understand.
He said: Understand what?
She said: That I'm not good at servitude.

He said: You're wasting my efforts.
She said: No, but I am asking you to change your crutch.
He said: My crutch?
She said: To set my feet free.

# The Cake

He said: Make the child be quiet. His crying is giving me a headache.

She said: Wait until the cake I'm making for him is finished.

He said: Hit him, scold him, shut him up any way you can—I'm tired.

She said: He's tired, too; he's waited a long time for this one simple thing he wants.

He said: You, an educated, cultured woman, are raising our child to think that his every wish should be accommodated, even at the expense of our nerves?

She said: And at the expense of his nerves...

He said: What does this child know about nerves and exhaustion?

She said: He knows more than you and more than me.

He said: Then I'll cry and scream to convince you I'm tired.

She said: You won't cry or scream. You know that you aren't capable of that.

He said: Are you challenging me?

She said: No...but I am speaking to you in plain speech.

He said: Are you going to allow a small child to give me a headache and forbid me to protest?

She said: How do you plan to protest?

He said: My voice is louder than his.

She said: I dare you to cry louder than him, go ahead!

He said: I will! Who will stop me?

She said: Everything around you...Accepted notions and common practices and basic principles and people's opinions...

He said: What is this, a blockade you're building around me?

She said: It's not me building the blockade...it's your sense of manhood.

He said: That's true, crying and screaming is for women and children.

She said: It's true, but not in the way that you think.

He said: Women's tears and the children's stubbornness are potent things.

She said: No one resorts to tears unless they feel they've been wronged or denied their needs, so what do you do if you feel that way?

He said: Isn't the cake ready?

She said: It's getting there.

He said: The child is quiet for a time, then stomps his feet demanding something else and you give it to him because you're afraid of a new tantrum.

She said: It's not my fear, it's his right. Only children have a right to protest, so why not give them their rights? No one would behave like this unless they felt that they had been mistreated.

He said: Then what can we adults do when we feel mistreated?

She said: We're quiet, silent, we stifle desires, they grow within us, and our nerves fall apart…

He screamed: Please…Please…It's just a cake.

She said: Yes, and I have to finish it and give it to our child to make him happy.

He said: And how do I become happy?

She said: You won't ever be happy as long as you're a person with wishes to which no one acknowledges your rights.

He said: I'm about to go crazy…I can hardly breathe…Don't talk to me about rights!

She said: Then agree with me. Isn't it our duty to give in to the wishes of children because children are able to express their needs?

He said: And be happy with their happiness and forget our own desires?

She said: No…We can't forget them, but unfortunately we can't cry or scream or threaten or…

He said: You encourage our child to behave badly, you teach him how to control us.

She said: I haven't taught him that and I won't teach him that. He knows instinctively. We adults know, too, but we can't act foolishly. So why stifle his rights?

He said: There's no need to remind me that I'm no longer a child with rights. I've grown up and been beaten.

She said: Your candor is frightening. You shouldn't reveal it to anyone, just let it be a secret between us.

He said: Isn't the cake done yet?

She said: Who abused you today?

He said: How did you know that I've been treated badly? How?

She said: Abused people take out their anger on the first weak person they meet.

He said: They dropped my name from the delegation.

She said: They dropped it? What about the paper you spent so many nights preparing?

He said: The new president of the delegation will present it and take credit for it.

She said: That's unfair! It's cruel! It's wicked!

He said: Bring the cake and give it quickly to our child.

She said: He's fallen asleep despite his tears and waiting, and I forgot the cake and let it burn.

He said: My anger burned the cake. And injustice put our neglected child to sleep.

She said: Your mistreatment sparked your anger. Why didn't you tell me about it, instead of letting me go on about simple things?

He said: Our child became the scapegoat.

She said: Be quiet now and let's try to forget.

He said: How can I forget? How can I forget the offense that's been done to me?

She said: If you don't try to put it aside, your anger will explode even more and its fire will spread.

He said: Yes, and all the cakes will be in danger of burning.

## DATE DUE

| | |
|---|---|
| | |
| | |
| | |
| | |
| | |
| | |
| | |
| | |
| | |
| | |
| | |
| | |
| | |
| | |
| | |
| | |
| | |
| | |
| | |
| | |
| | |
| | |
| GAYLORD | PRINTED IN U.S.A. |